For Clara.
Great friends make everything better.
—C.L.

To Jen R.
A truly, truly, truly good friend.
—M.P.

STERLING CHILDREN'S BOOKS
New York

An Imprint of Sterling Publishing
387 Park Avenue South
New York, NY 10016

STERLING CHILDREN'S BOOKS and the distinctive Sterling Children's Books logo are trademarks of
Sterling Publishing Co., Inc.

© 2013 by Cynthea Liu
Illustrations © 2013 by Mary Peterson
Cover and interior design by Jennifer Browning
The illustrations in this book were drawn in pencil by hand and then painted digitally.

ISBN 978-1-4027-9644-9

Library of Congress Cataloging-in-Publication Data

Liu, Cynthea.
  Wooby & Peep / by Cynthea Liu ; illustrated by Mary Peterson.
    p. cm.
  Summary: When Peep leaves the city to live in the country with her pet iguana, her new neighbor, Wooby, is concerned
but tries to be polite and neighborly, even when her efforts to become his friend lead to disaster.
  ISBN 978-1-4027-9644-9
  [1. Neighbors--Fiction. 2. Moving, Household--Fiction. 3. Bears--Fiction. 4. Birds--Fiction. 5. Forest animals--Fiction.] I.
Peterson, Mary, ill. II. Title. III. Title: Wooby & Peep.
  PZ7.L739325Woo 2013
  [E]--dc23

2012015827

Distributed in Canada by Sterling Publishing
c/o Canadian Manda Group, 165 Dufferin Street
Toronto, Ontario, Canada M6K 3H6
Distributed in the United Kingdom by GMC Distribution Services
Castle Place, 166 High Street, Lewes, East Sussex, England BN7 1XU
Distributed in Australia by Capricorn Link (Australia) Pty. Ltd.
P.O. Box 704, Windsor, NSW 2756, Australia

For information about custom editions, special sales, and premium and corporate purchases, please contact
Sterling Special Sales at 800-805-5489 or specialsales@sterlingpublishing.com.

Manufactured in China
Lot #:
2 4 6 8 10 9 7 5 3 1
11/12

www.sterlingpublishing.com/kids

Wooby & Peep

A Story
of Unlikely
Friendship

by
Cynthea Liu

illustrations by
Mary Peterson

Wooby loved his goldfish, Wendy, and his humble home. He lived on a quiet little street where the neighbors minded their own business.

Until one day . . .

Peep moved in.

"Wow, Ricardo," Peep said. "Smell that air. Listen to that quiet. It's not like the city, is it? You think the neighbors will mind my sound system?"

Wooby swallowed. "Wendy, I hope this isn't as bad as it looks."

The next day, the whole neighborhood was invited
to Peep's housewarming party.
Wooby and Wendy gulped.

"A wild party?" Wooby asked. "I'm not the wild type, but it
would be rude if we didn't go. Right, Wendy?"

The other neighbors suddenly had plans. They liked their neighborhood just the way it was, and Peep's party sounded so . . . *different.*

I've got work to do.	That's my day to bunnysit.	What about my mud bath?	"When Animals Attack" will be on.
I'm allergic. Achoo!	Who has time to monkey around?	Neigh.	Bah!
Wild? I don't do wild.	That's when I meditate.	Oh, dear.	Got a match that night.
Whoooose party is it?	I'm alphabetizing my nut collection that day.	That's when I have moo-sic lessons!	I need to go potty.

The big day finally arrived and Peep's party was a stunning . . . failure. Nobody came except Wooby and Wendy.

"Would you like to pin the tail on the zebra? Want to take a jungle ride? Or maybe we can do a safari dance?" Peep asked.

"Sounds like fun . . . but . . . um . . . no, thanks," Wooby said.

The party had been a flop, but Peep was not a quitter. She wanted to be Wooby's friend.

The next day, Peep called to her neighbor. "It's a truly, truly, truly terrific day to do something nice for a friend, wouldn't you say?"

"Sure, Peep." Wooby listened to his fountain and read a comic book.

547 year old tree
—
Do Not Lean!

Trickle, Trickle, Trickle!

After Wooby cleaned up the mess, he trimmed his
magnificent maple.

That Peep sure is interesting, he thought.

Next door, Peep was busy fixing Wooby's favorite
flowing fountain.

The next morning, Wooby planted petunias in his
prized petunia patch.

He sang them a glorious tune. *"Petunias, petunias.
It's so nice to grow ya's—"*

Suddenly, Wooby heard Peep yell from next door.
Peep was up to something. Again.

"This new forest will make Wooby forget about his maple tree," Peep said.

It was perfectly quiet.

Or maybe, just maybe, a little too quiet . . . and lonely?

"We're not lonely, are we?" Wooby asked Wendy.

Wendy's brow furrowed.

"I agree. Not lonely at all," Wooby said unconvincingly.
"We're *fine*."

Suddenly, more noises came from next door.

"What is Peep doing *now*?" Wooby asked.

Wooby stomped over to
Peep's house and flung open the
door. There was Peep. And
Ricardo. And a giant mess.

"What are you doing, Peep?" Wooby asked.

"I'm trying to make everything up to you. I'm sorry for ruining your house, your fountain, your tree . . . . Did you know that tree was 547 years old?! *Wah!*"

Wooby softened. "*Peep...*"

"I just wanted to thank you for being my friend," Peep said.

"Your friend?" Wooby scratched his head. "I'm just a *neighbor*, Peep." He sighed.

WONDER WOMBAT

SPIDER CAT

Batdog & Robin

"No, you're not," Peep replied.
"You came to my party. You were the only
one, and this whole time I've just wanted
to be a friend back. I was sooo lonely.
No offense, Ricardo."

Lonely? Wooby thought.

"And do you have any idea how hard
it is to play Go Fish with an iguana?
No offense again, Ricardo."

"You play

Go Fish,

too?"

"Let's be friends," Wooby said.

"Truly, truly, truly?" Peep asked.
"Of course!" Wooby replied.

Wooby and Peep made big plans for a party.

It was a housebuilding party.

Glide,
glide.

Break
it down.

Slide, slide.

A party for two.
"Just you and me," Wooby said.
"Wooby and Peep!" Peep said.
"Best friends forever!"

NEW
Magnificent
Maple

BUS
STOP